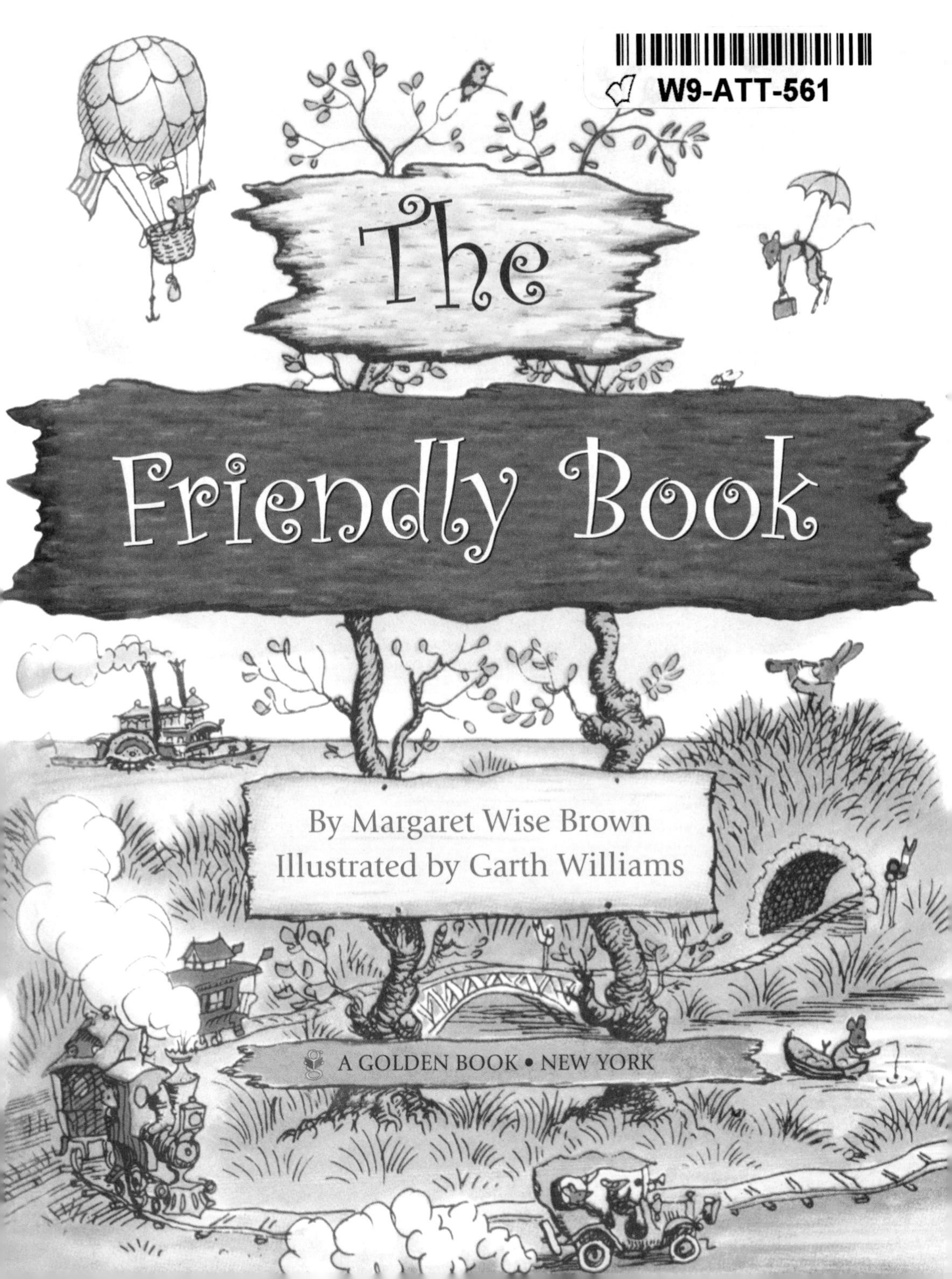
The
Friendly Book
By Margaret Wise Brown
Illustrated by Garth Williams
A GOLDEN BOOK • NEW YORK

Published in the United States by Golden Books, an imprint of Random House Children's Books, a division of Random House, Inc., 1745 Broadway, New York, NY 10019. Originally published in slightly different form in the United States by Simon and Schuster, Inc., and Artists and Writers Guild, Inc., in 1954.
www.randomhouse.com/kids
Educators and librarians, for a variety of teaching tools, visit us at
www.randomhouse.com/teachers
Library of Congress Control Number: 2011925344
ISBN: 978-0-307-92962-4
Printed in the United States of America
10 9 8 7 6 5

I LIKE CARS

Red cars Green cars

Sport limousine cars

I like cars
A car in a garage
A car with a load
A car with a flat tire
A car on the road
I like cars.

TOURS
HILL
STOP

I LIKE TRAINS

Express trains
Toy trains
Streamline trains
Freight trains
Old trains
Milk trains

4073
6076
6076
3
3

Any kind of train
A train in the station
Trains crossing the plains

Trains in a snowstorm
Trains in the rain
I like trains.

CONDU
Mr BARK

STARSHIP

I LIKE STARS

Yellow stars
Green stars
Red stars
Blue stars
I like stars
Far stars
Quiet stars
Bright stars
Light stars
I like stars
A star that is shooting across the dark sky
A star that is shining right straight in your eye
I like stars.

I LIKE SNOW

Cold snow
Slow snow
White snow
Icy snow
I like snow
Snow falling softly with everything still
White in the blue night, white on the sill
White on the trees on the far distant hill
With everything still
I like snow.

I LIKE FISH

Silver fish Gold fish
Black fish Old fish
Young fish Fishy fish
Any kind of fish

A fish in a pond
A fish in a stream
A fish in the ocean
A fish in a dream
I like fish.

I LIKE DOGS

Big dogs Little dogs
Fat dogs Doggy dogs
Old dogs Puppy dogs

ICES
SALE
CIGARS
CIGARETTES
SODA
SODA
HOT! DOGS 10¢
BONES
FRESH FRANKS
POLICE

I like dogs
A dog that is barking over the hill
A dog that is dreaming very still
A dog that is running wherever he will
I like dogs.

I LIKE BOATS

Any kind of boat

Tug boats Tow boats

Large boats Barge boats

Sail boats Whale boats
Thin boats Skin boats
Rubber boats River boats
Flat boats Cat boats
U boats New boats

Tooting boats Hooting boats
South American fruit boats
Bum boats Gun boats
Slow boats Row boats
I like boats.

I LIKE PEOPLE

Glad people
Sad people
Slow people
Mad people
Big people
Little people

I like people.